Bob Cratchit's
Christmas
Carol

The Untold Miracle of Charles Dickens's Classic

Leonard Szymczak

GPS BOOKS

Praise for
Bob Cratchit's
Christmas
Carol

"*Bob Cratchit's Christmas Carol* will inspire you to let go of the past, awaken your true purpose, and create miracles."

— Jack Canfield, *New York Times* bestselling
author of *The Success Principles*™ and cocreator
of the *Chicken Soup for the Soul*® series

"Leonard Szymczak presents a superbly resonant, intelligent, and charming addition to the Dickens classic, and one which celebrates the original style and atmosphere of Dickens himself but also seeks to convey more complex messages about the nature of happiness."

— Readers' Favorite®

"Scrooge's poor and dispirited clerk takes center stage as we watch the Christmas Spirits arrive in the most compelling angels ever to grace a page, angels that present our hero with his own Christmas past, present, and future, teaching us that our lives are not just precious, but to be lived in the fullest expression of love and love's close companion, joy. Bob Cratchit's story is ultimately as fun as that last giant colorfully wrapped present under the tree."

~ JJ Flowers, award-winning author of *Juan
Pablo and the Butterflies* and *Grief Is Love.*

"That master weaver of stories, Leonard Szymczak, gave us another wonderful page turner. What's more fun than reading a Christmas story with a message of love and forgiveness?"

~ Danna Beal, author of *The Extraordinary Workplace: Replacing Fear with Trust and Compassion*

"In *Bob Cratchit's Christmas Carol* we rediscover ourselves alongside Bob Cratchit as he journeys through the hours of Christmas Eve. With each lesson he's shown a mirror for us to digest our own mistakes, missteps, and triumphs. The prose acts as an arrow that pierces our heart to unlock the reason why we live. A skillful and mystical take on a traditional tale each one of us needs to read."

~ Jennifer Myers, author of *Trafficking the Good Life*

"As a lifelong Dickens's fan, especially of *A Christmas Carol*, I've been enchanted by the different iterations of this story. Leonard's continuation of this tale, bringing Bob Cratchit to life in a way Dickens would have loved, gives another dimension to this story, one that is vibrantly realistic and delightfully hopeful."

~ Mary Harris, author of *Diggz and Wrrrussell* series

"A beautiful addition to the classic story. It turns out gentle Bob Cratchit has lessons to learn as well, lessons that will ring true for many readers today."

~ Brandon Hall, co-author with Jack Canfield and Janet Switzer of *The Success Principles Workbook*

"*Bob Cratchit's Christmas Carol* is a heartwarming twist on Charles Dickens's 1843 novella. Leonard blends his deep understanding of spirituality and psychology to transform Scrooge's abused, underpaid clerk. When Bob is visited by angelic beings, he recognizes his true essence so he can love, forgive, and be empowered to release his own pain and feelings of lack."

~ Mari Frank, author of *From Victim to Victor*, *Safeguard Your Identity*, and coauthor of *Fighting for Love: Turn Conflict into Intimacy*

"This guy can turn an ancient story into one for our age and beyond. This master wrote another one!"

~ Kevin E. O'Connor, CSP, author with Cyndi Maxey, CSP of *Present Like a Pro: The Field Guide to Mastering the Art of Business, Professional, and Public Speaking*

"Leonard Szymczak has written a delightful and moving variation of *A Christmas Carol* that brings the lessons of Christmas Past, Present, and Future into the 21st century. In this tale, Bob Cratchit receives powerful lessons from three earnest female ghosts who help him realize his own Christmas Miracle. Bob's life is changed forever as he discovers how to let go of past wounds, release his fear, embrace love, and go for his dreams. This story is a heartwarming update that any reader, young or old, will find inspiring and well worth reading!"

~ Rick Broniec, author of *A Passionate Life* and the Amazon bestselling *The Seven Generations Story*

"A must read for fans of Charles Dickens. A new twist on a famous tale that you'll be a scrooge to miss."

"Leonard has an exceptional gift of imagination and telling stories that allow us to envision the characters, places, and the happenings in a unique way. I know *Bob Cratchit's Christmas Carol* will intrigue you and have you engaged with the characters and their roles with a new and delightful perspective."

"Prepare a mug of smoking bishop and snuggle down into your comfortable recliner. Then, enjoy a more profound, many-sided world of the *Christmas Carol*. Charles Dickens told us what happened on Christmas Eve in the early 1800s. Leonard begins his novella much as Dickens did in a rendition of the counting-house. But then Szymczak curves away from Dickens, builds momentum, then bends back around to the initial Dickens's story."

Other Books by Leonard Szymczak

The Roadmap Home: Your GPS to Inner Peace

Cuckoo Forevermore

Kookaburra's Last Laugh

Fighting for Love: Turn Conflict into Intimacy
Coauthored with Mari Frank

This is a work of fiction. It draws upon some of
the names, characters, and events as portrayed
in *A Christmas Carol* by Charles Dickens.

Library of Congress Control Number: 2021918690

Author: Szymczak, Leonard

Title: *Bob Cratchit's Christmas Carol: The Untold
Miracle of Charles Dickens's Classic*

Published by GPS Books, Dana Point, California, 92629

ISBN – 13: 978-0-9969566-6-6 (paperback)
ISBN – 13: 978-0-9969566-7-3 (e-book)
ISBN – 13: 978-0-9969566-8-0 (hardback)

Cover Design: Fiona Jayde
Interior Design: Tamara Cribley
Editors: Mary Harris & Glenda Rynn
Author of "Artwork" by work made
for hire: Leonard Szymczak
Author Photo: Esperanza H.S. Photography Department

Printed in the United States of America

1. Fiction/Holidays. 2. Fiction/Christian/Classic & Allegory.

"Our life is what our thoughts make it."

~ Marcus Aurelius

Chapter One

Scrooge and Marley's Ghost

On Christmas Eve, 1843, in a rundown part of London, a solitary man, wearing a tattered coat, scribbled in a ledger. Bob Cratchit shivered in his tiny office, which felt more like his prison cell. Lit by a sole candle and furnished with a rickety wooden chair and a scruffy desk, the office had a small fireplace. Bob had to nurse his daily allotment of coal which barely warmed the fireplace throughout the cold winter's day. He dared not use more than one lump of coal at a time, for his miserly employer complained bitterly that he wasted precious fuel.

Cratchit, a small man with unkempt black hair and muttonchop sideburns, glanced through the open doorway into the larger office where his employer sat behind a dark mahogany desk, gleefully counting gold coins. Though his fireplace burned with a few more lumps of coal, Ebenezer Scrooge never indulged in excess. He painfully managed his wealth and possessions, down to a bucket of coal. A coldhearted man, he seemed to prefer a frosty room.

When it came to other's needs, Scrooge never wasted. Having his clerk stay warm seemed a total waste. Besides, if Cratchit shivered, he would work harder to keep warm. According to Scrooge, too much comfort weakened the will. He peered through the doorway that he kept open to spy on his clerk. No dawdling on his time.

"Cratchit!" growled the gnarled man who was hard as flint. "Finish those papers and complete the ledger before you leave."

Bob stopped warming his fingers over the candle. "Yes, Mr. Scrooge," he whimpered. He blew into his hands, grasped the ink pen, and scribbled on the page.

At this time each year, the accounting had to be complete before Cratchit could leave for the day. Since Scrooge hated Christmas and paying his clerk for a holiday, he piled on extra work to make up for it. As a result, Christmas Eve became Bob Cratchit's longest day. His wife would be lucky to see him before the church bells tolled nine times.

Bob dipped his pen in the ink and sighed. He had toiled and slaved for the miserly man for the past twenty years. The work had become more unbearable when Scrooge's partner, Jacob Marley, died seven years ago. Though Marley was just as greedy as Scrooge, he had assisted Bob with the bookkeeping. Once Scrooge was on his own, he piled Marley's duties onto Cratchit's growing list of chores—without a raise. The clerk was still making fifteen shillings a week.

Bob had once hoped to be rewarded for his diligence and loyalty. Those dreams had vanished years ago. Though he yearned to work elsewhere, he felt shackled to Scrooge. He had to support a wife and six children, and the youngest child Tiny Tim desperately needed medical treatment.

Each year Bob begged for a raise, but nothing could stir the embers in Scrooge's frozen heart. When money entered his vault, it was locked away until he could lend it to an unfortunate soul at an exorbitant rate. As a moneylender, he was despised for extracting severe penalties for non-payment, no matter how unfortunate the situation.

And situations always presented themselves.

Rap. Rap. Rap.

At noon on Christmas Eve, Mrs. Dibble had arrived for her appointment. Responding to the knock on the door, Bob ushered her out of the blistering cold and into his employer's office. They both stood before Scrooge who, not raising an eyebrow, continued to count coins and scribble into a notebook.

"Excuse me, Mr. Scrooge," squeaked Bob.

"Yes, what is it?" growled Scrooge, continuing to write.

Cratchit nudged the frail woman who smelled as if she had not bathed in a month. She clutched her tattered clothes which looked more like rags. "Ye'll beg me pardon, Mr. Scrooge," she quivered. "I didn't want to disturb ye, but I need to have a word about the loan."

The last word acted like a magic incantation that woke Scrooge from a trance. He dropped his pen and gazed intensely at the woman. "Loan, you say? You've come to repay your loan? You're late."

Mrs. Dibble lowered her eyes to the floor. "Ye know me husband's recovering from a heart ailment. Can't yet walk… or work. I'm takin' in laundry and doin' odd jobs to pay the bills. It's… just… we need more time."

Scrooge leaned back in his wooden chair and squinted his eyes menacingly. "Time, you say? The last time you were here, you begged for mercy. I gave you two months' extension—with added interest."

"Me husband can't walk, Mr. Scrooge," whimpered Mrs. Dibble with tears trickling down her cheek.

Bob whispered, "Can we give her a little more time, Mr. Scrooge? 'Tis Christmas."

"Bah, humbug, Cratchit," ranted Scrooge. "I don't run a charity. Having you work for me is charity enough! Write in the ledger that the Dibbles defaulted on their loan. Draw up the papers. I'll take possession of their shabby house."

"No, Mr. Scrooge!" sobbed Mrs. Dibble. "What about me children?" She dabbed her eyes with a dirty hanky. "We have nowhere to go."

"You should have thought about that when your husband asked for a loan. You signed a document. It says that when you don't pay the loan, I take your house." He pointed to the door and glared at Cratchit. "See her out!"

The old woman touched the lender's arm and screeched, "Please, Mr. Scrooge. Have mercy."

Scrooge recoiled at the woman's touch, as if she had a contagious disease. "Out," he yelled. "Cratchit, take her away!"

Bob glanced apologetically at Mrs. Dibble, whose body shook uncontrollably. With thoughts of being thrown out in the cold with an ailing husband and four children, she buried her face into her hands and wept. He gently took her arm and guided her out of the room. He reached into his pocket and handed her a coin, the money he had saved to purchase chocolate as a Christmas treat for his family.

Mrs. Dibble stared at the coin and wiped tears from her eyes. She then placed it in her pocket and said, "Bless ye, kind sir." She kissed Bob's cheek then scurried out of the building into the freezing wind.

"Close the door, Cratchit! We're not here to heat all of London."

With a heavy heart, Bob returned to his desk. How many times had he wanted to shout, "*Scoundrel, sinner! I'll work no more for you.*"

But he always stopped himself. He desperately needed a job to care for his wife and six children. He was heavily in debt, having borrowed money to treat Tiny Tim's failing body. Without proper care, his youngest son, who needed metal braces and crutches to help him walk, had little chance of surviving another year.

Bob returned to his desk and dipped his pen in the ink. He glanced towards Scrooge, who wore a perpetual scowl. Unmarried, his employer hated people and hated losing money. But he especially hated Christmas. He also hated the idea that upon his death his money would be dispersed to his foolish nephew, the only surviving relative.

It wasn't long before his nephew appeared for his annual Christmas Eve visit. The handsome, robust man threw open the door. Flushed by his brisk walk, Fred bustled into the room.

He took off his hat and nodded cheerfully to Bob. "Merry Christmas, my good man."

"Merry Christmas," replied Bob. "Always good to see you."

Fred strolled into Scrooge's office, "And may you have a merry Christmas, Uncle!"

"Bah," said Scrooge. "Humbug."

"Humbug on Christmas, Uncle? You always say that."

"Because I mean it," grumbled Scrooge. "You have no reason to be merry."

"I am not wealthy like you but find plenty to be merry about. With all your wealth, you should have plenty reason to be merry."

"Bah. Humbug. I have no time to talk of merriment like you fools. Christmas should be banned, and everyone who celebrates it should be boiled with his own pudding."

"Uncle, please. The Spirit of Christmas beckons us all to bring peace to the world. Surely, you wouldn't deprive us of that joy?"

"I'll treat Christmas as any other day on the calendar, even if I have to pay a clerk's wages for work undone." Scrooge cast an evil glance at Bob who held his quill in the air while he eavesdropped on the conversation. "You'll be working overtime today, Cratchit."

"Don't be angry, Uncle," pleaded his nephew. "Come dine with me and my wife this evening. You still haven't met her."

"I don't have time for such foolishness. Why did you ever get married?"

"Because I fell in love."

"Love? Humbug. Makes a man soft." He glanced down at the coins on his desk. "The only thing of value is money."

"I am a rich man."

Scrooge gazed intently at his nephew. "How and when have you come to be so rich?"

"I may not have your gold coins, but I have a wife and friends who make me feel very rich, indeed."

"Spoken by someone who has little wealth."

Fred's smile faded. "Money has not brought you happiness, Uncle."

"I survive and grow my business. That's all I need."

"I have never asked anything for myself," said his nephew. "I have honored your sister, my dead mother, and her wishes to treat you kindly. I did not hold a grudge when you refused to attend my wedding. And though you have declined my offer every year, I still extend the invitation to dine with us tomorrow."

Scrooge waved his hands as if shooing away flies. "Away. I have pressing work."

"Like every Christmas?"

"Good afternoon," said Scrooge.

"Can we not be friends, my dear uncle?"

"Good afternoon!" Scrooge picked up his quill and began scribbling on a page. "Cratchit, show my nephew out."

Fred sighed and left the room. He stopped by Bob's desk and offered his hand. "I wish you and your family a merry Christmas."

"Out," cried Scrooge, pointing toward the door. He stabbed a gnarly finger at the pendulum clock ticking away on the wall behind him. "You're wasting my clerk's time."

As the nephew placed his hat on his head, Bob whispered, "Merry Christmas, kind sir." Fred nodded and hurried out of the office into the freezing cold.

No sooner had Bob returned to work when he was startled by yet another knocking on the door. *Rap, rap, rap.*

Bob nervously opened the wooden door. He found two well-dressed, portly men, one with sagging jowls and the other with snow-white hair. They bowed and asked to speak with Mr. Scrooge.

"This is not a good time," whispered Bob.

They moved into the room. "Nonsense," announced the older man rather cheerfully. "We have a marvelous proposal."

"I… I don't know," stammered Bob.

Both men handed him their hats and walked into Scrooge's office.

"Good day, Mr. Scrooge," announced Augustus Jingle. "I'm here with Alfred Bell, and we bring a wonderful offer."

Scrooge gazed at them. "What's the meaning of this?" he announced angrily. He spotted his clerk in the background. "Why did you let them in?"

Before Bob could answer, Augustus stepped forward, "We're here with a proposal."

"Proposal? What kind of proposal?"

With sagging jowls, Alfred Bell smiled at his partner who nodded for him to continue. "My friend and I are purchasing food for the children in the orphanage so they can enjoy Christmas like the rest of us. We propose that you support our cause."

Scrooge spat on the floor. "I don't support vermin."

Alfred remained undeterred and continued to smile. "Well-fed children make for productive children."

"Why should I give them food? They have poor houses, don't they?"

"Why, yes."

"Let *them* care for your children. That is their business, not mine."

Augustus intervened. "Excuse me, Mr. Scrooge. We believe you to be a decent fellow."

"We are all good underneath," added Alfred. "We can make the world a better place, but we need your help." He pointed to the coins on the desk. "A few of those will feed some hungry children."

The miser clutched the coins closer to him. "I'm not a charity."

"Can you not spare something for the poor?"

Rubbing his pointed chin, Scrooge smirked. "Why, yes… I think I can offer you something."

Augustus nodded to his friend. "I knew he would help." He turned to Scrooge. "How much can we count on?"

Standing up from his desk, Scrooge moved to the fireplace and dipped his hand into a bucket. "One piece of coal should do." He plucked a chunk of black coal and tossed it to Augustus. It bounced off his snow-white hair, leaving a dark smudge.

"You have my contribution. Now leave!"

He pushed his chair to the side. "Cratchit, show them out. And after they leave, don't let anyone else in, or *you* will be out of a job."

The two men, frozen by the outburst, stared at each other.

"Quit dawdling, Cratchit! Show them the door."

The older man picked up the chunk of coal off the floor and placed it on the desk. "You need this to warm your heart. Good day, sir."

Followed by Alfred Bell, Augustus Jingle hurried to the front door where they gathered their hats. They said no more and left without a smile.

Scrooge shook his head in disgust. "Another wasted moment."

When Bob closed the door, he returned to his books, hoping for no more interruptions. With quill in hand, he checked his watch — half past five. He would be late again for Christmas Eve.

Scrooge placed the coins in a drawer and locked it. "I have one more debt to collect," he announced. "Another idle man spends my money. I will give him a Christmas present he will never forget."

"What will that be, Mr. Scrooge?" asked his clerk, hoping beyond hope for a change of heart.

"The last time, the scoundrel begged for mercy." He cackled. "I showed him mercy and charged him double interest. Now, I'll take possession of his house."

Horrified, Bob pleaded, "Can it not wait, Mr. Scrooge? 'Tis Christmas."

"Bah! Humbug!" He walked to the door. "Don't you dare leave until you've finished your work. Otherwise, I'll dock you the full day."

Bob handed him his coat and top hat. "I hope it won't be too much trouble, Mr. Scrooge, if I have Christmas off."

Scrooge stared at Bob's muttonchop sideburns as he put on his coat and sneered, "Every Christmas Eve, you ask the same. Why should I pay you for work you've never done?"

"Because it's Christmas?"

"Bah! Humbug!" shouted Scrooge. "It means nothing to me, except unearned wages."

Bob gave Scrooge his scarf. "I'll complete all the paperwork before I leave."

Scrooge wrapped his scarf around his neck and placed the top hat on his head. "See that you do," he growled. "And come to work extra early the day after Christmas."

He opened the door and stepped out of the counting house and into the freezing air, muttering, "Bah, humbug. Christmas!"

After he left, Bob breathed a sigh of relief. Though he would have to work late, he could do so in peace, away from the scornful eyes of a tyrant. He placed another piece of coal on the fireplace, warmed his hands over the candle, then worked feverishly, stopping periodically to warm his hands by the small fire.

He checked his watch—half past six. He rubbed his tired eyes and imagined the Christmas feast that would occur around midnight, a Cratchit tradition established because of Scrooge. Since the miser forced him to stay late every Christmas Eve, Bob's wife postponed the feast until after he finished work and had taken Tiny Tim to church.

He slowly brought his eyes to the papers on his desk. He had to complete the pile of work before he could leave. He nestled into his tattered coat and copied figures to a page.

Clink! Clank! Clang!

"Ebenezer, Ebenezer," cried a withered voice.

"Ahhhhh!" shrieked Bob. He backed away from the sickly apparition walking through the front door. Terrified of the ghost, Bob rubbed his eyes, hoping he had fallen asleep from fatigue and was having a nightmare.

Clink! Clank! Clang!

"Ebenezer," called the figure. His body was translucent, and he wore a heavy coat surrounded by chains and shackles.

Bob shivered at the phantom ghost. "Wh-who are y-you? Wh-what are you?"

"I am Jacob Marley."

"That can't be!" cried Bob. Scrooge's former partner had died seven years ago to the day!

"Look at me, Bob. You know who I am."

"I *am* having a nightmare," he told himself. He shook his head to clear his thoughts and blinked his eyes. He then pinched his cheek. *Ouch!*

The apparition remained in front of him. And he did, indeed, resemble the Jacob Marley who had established the lending business with Scrooge. The sign outside still read: *SCROOGE AND MARLEY*.

When the chained man edged closer to the clerk, Bob recoiled in fear. "S-stay away," he shuddered. "I'm a God-fearing man. You have no business with me."

Marley pointed a bony finger at the clerk. "I do have business today, Bob Cratchit. With Scrooge... and you! Like me, you have chained yourself to a money-grubbing man. You must find the key and release yourself or you will end up in chains, forever."

Bob whimpered, "By all means, visit Mr. Scrooge. He needs your guidance, not me. Please, sir, leave me be. I beg you!"

The apparition rattled his chains. "Scrooge will have his day, but you must unfetter your mind. I was chained to greed. You are chained to fear."

"No, no!" cried the clerk. "I do not fear that I will become like you and Scrooge. You had no family or friends. I love my wife and children. I have friends."

Marley cackled. "A loving family and friends, yes indeed. But still you are enslaved. You fear Ebenezer. You fear the loss of your job. You fear the dreams that haunt you while you sleep. You fear Tiny Tim's death."

He waved his transparent arms, sending the sound of clanking chains reverberating in the room. "You are enslaved like me."

Bob shook so badly he had to clutch the desktop. "'Tis true. But wh-what do you want?"

"Soon, I will give a message to Ebenezer, but you are in need of one as well."

"Wh-what message?"

"You will be visited by three Spirits. One from the past, another from the present and then one from the future. Listen to them. Release your shackles."

"No, sir. Please, send the Spirits to Scrooge. Give him the Christmas message!"

Marley bobbed his head. "He will meet his own Spirits soon enough." His face ghostly white, he drifted closer. "Do you wish to walk through life burdened by fear and forsaken dreams?"

Bob shook his wobbling head. "That is my fate, sir. I am a poor and simple man. I bear my weight well."

Marley cackled. "You are poor but not as you believe. Sleep now until the first Spirit arrives."

Waving his clanking hand towards the clerk, the ghost disappeared through the front door. Bob blinked several times as if in a stupor. He felt a crushing weight on his shoulders. What Marley said was true. He was chained to a poor, wretched life. Fearful of losing his job, he had toiled day after day for the past twenty years for a man who squeezed the joy out of his life. He hated the abuse, but fearing he would lose his job, he saw little choice but to suffer and survive. His family had to be sheltered and fed. Tiny Tim needed proper treatment, but already burdened by debt, Bob could no longer afford doctors.

If truth be told, Bob hated his life. While he loved his wife and six children, he saw himself as a failure, unable to provide a good life for them. He fell into periods of deep despair, feeling hopeless and powerless. He tried to put on a happy face to protect his family from his misery, but they sensed his broken spirit.

Bob placed his weary head on the desk, hoping Marley's visit was an aberration and would fade from his memory. Fatigue overtook him. He soon fell into a deep slumber.

Chapter Two

The First Spirit

*D*ing, dong. Ding, dong. Ding…

As the wall clock in Scrooge's office struck seven, Bob felt a tug at his arm. He screamed, thinking it was Jacob Marley.

Instead of Scrooge's partner, Bob saw a tall, vivacious woman with ebony skin, dressed in a flowing red dress decorated with evergreen garlands. A bright aura surrounded her angelic face, and little bells woven into her beaded black hair tinkled as she spoke. She tapped him with a branch of fresh green holly. "Wake up. I am here to spirit you away to the past."

"The p-past! Why?" quivered the clerk. He rubbed his eyes hoping the apparition would disappear.

She reached out her hand. "Come."

"Wh-who are you?"

"I am the Spirit of Christmas Past." Exuding a scent of pine, she moved closer to the terrified man. "You can call me Angelica. I'm here to show you what you have forgotten."

Bob did not want to visit the forgotten. He wanted to finish his work and rush home to the comforting arms of his wife and children.

As if reading his mind, Angelica said, "You will be home soon enough. For now, you must look within. The past haunts you."

Bob cringed. "Why must I visit the past? 'Tis already done."

The Spirit shook her head, causing the bells to tinkle. "The past is very much alive."

Glancing at the papers on his desk, he protested, "I must finish these before I can leave."

"Child's play," she tittered. "Leave your desk and grab hold of this branch."

Treating the branch as if it was a viper, he cowered against the wall. He shut his eyes, hoping he was dreaming and would soon wake up.

Waking up is what the Spirit had in mind. She waved the holly. A scent of pine wafted in the air, calming Bob's nerves. He opened his eyes and, ever so reluctantly, grabbed hold of the outstretched holly, whereupon he was transported into a milky mist. His body began to spin in a counterclockwise fashion until he finally came to a dizzying stop. When the mist faded, he found himself standing alongside Angelica in snow, though he, himself, did not feel the cold. Standing nearby was a ten-year-old boy shivering by the side of an icy road, selling papers.

Bob turned to the Spirit. "Can he see us?"

She shook her head. "We are invisible. Watch and learn."

An angry, gaunt man wearing a filthy shirt and torn pants strides up to the boy and grabs his papers. He tosses them on the road and yells, "Come, boy!"

"But, Father," says the son, "I earned some coins."

"Hand them over, boy," yells his father. "I need money. I'll have you workin' at Warren's Blacking Warehouse. They'll give you food and shelter and give me two shillings a week — as long as you work hard."

Smelling whiskey on his father's breath, the boy pleads, "I can do better than labeling pots of shoe polish. And Mother needs my help." He glances at the papers on the road. "I'll sell other things to earn money."

"I need money now!" admonishes his father. He slaps the boy across the side of the head. "Do as I say."

His son stares down at his worn pants and then at his toes poking out of the holes on his shoes. He glances at his father's dirty threadbare clothes. "I want something better than what we have."

"You have a knack with numbers. I'll give you that. With any luck, they'll let you do the ledgers. Let's go."

The boy gazes at the ground. Not daring to look at his father, he mumbles, "I don't want to be poor. I dream about making lots of money and helping others."

His father swats him again, knocking him to the ground. "Get that stupid idea out of your sick head. Do as I say, boy."

Bob cringed at the sight of his younger self. "Spirit, I don't need to see anymore. That past is forgotten. I no longer wish to be reminded of it."

The tall Spirit shook her head, causing the bells interlaced in her black hair to tinkle. "Your mind carries memories like a book. You may have forgotten the pages, but they shape your life. Your past plagues the present. You must recognize that before you can choose another future."

"But I no longer think of the past," protested Bob.

"The past is very much alive in your mind. Come," smiled Angelica. "There is more to see." She swished her red dress, causing the evergreen garlands to sparkle. "Take hold," she said, offering the branch of holly.

Grateful to leave the scene with his father, Bob did as instructed. Immediately, he was whisked away to another setting—Warren's Blacking Warehouse. He winced when he spotted Uriah Quilp sauntering towards his younger self, now eleven, sitting on a stool in front of a bench where a row of children pasted labels on pots of shoe polish.

Holding a long stick, the cruel man smacks one of the children across the shoulder. "No dawdling."

Uriah lashes out at another lad who has fallen behind on his quota. As he moves up the row of children, he spots Bob gawking at him. "Cratchit. Did I give you permission to stop working?"

"No, sir," shudders the young boy, his face and fingers smudged with polish.

The stick crashes across his stooped shoulder. When the boy cries out in pain, he receives another blow.

"Spirit, take me away," screamed Bob recoiling, bending his shoulder as if he had been beaten. "I cannot bear this."

"There is more to learn."

Bob pleaded, "I've endured much pain in the past. It haunts me still, but there's nothing I can do. Do not force me to remember."

Angelica pointed the branch at Uriah Quilp. "Does he not remind you of someone? Do you not live every day with the fear of being beaten down by Scrooge?"

Turning away, Bob clutched his trembling body. "Yes, but I must provide for my family."

"But you repeat the past."

"I cannot change that."

"Like Jacob Marley, you are chained to the past. You live in your memories and recreate them — with different characters, yes, but with similar outcomes."

"There is nothing I can do," protested Bob meekly.

"I show you the past so you learn from it and let it go."

"How can I let go of so much pain? When I turned fifteen, I visited my father on his deathbed. The whiskey killed him. He left my dear mother in the poorhouse and my brother and sisters in workhouses. The last thing he told me was to work for the rich, steal when you can, and forget the nonsense about dreaming of a better life. I followed his advice—except for stealing."

Angelica nodded causing the bells to tinkle once more. "You learned to survive but you let the past stop you from living."

"I had no choice."

"You are choosing to sleepwalk through life. I have come to awaken you."

"You want to wake me to my pain?"

"I want you to awaken and heal the past."

"This is beyond my understanding."

The Spirit tapped him on the crown of his head with the branch of holly, causing the scent of pine to permeate the air. "You are born to experience life in many ways," she said. "But you are not meant to hold onto them. You are meant to learn from your experiences, bless them, then let them go."

Bob rubbed his shoulder where he had once felt the lashings from Uriah Quilp. "Some things I cannot let go."

"Unless you release the pain, you will bring the same emotions back to you, again and again. Do you not do so with Scrooge?"

He protested, "I must feed my family."

"Feed them, yes. But do so while awake."

Bob shook his confused head. "Your visitation could be nothing but a nightmare."

"This is no nightmare," said Angelica. "I have come to show you how to be fully awake. Let me explain. Whenever you think of winter, you think of snow and the cold. That is your reality because you have experienced winter only in England. Imagine that you sailed to a tropical island. Would you try and convince the islanders that they should be cold in the winter? The islanders who experience winter as sunny and warm would think you mad if you suggested otherwise."

Angelica's body began to glow, radiating light and heat from her ebony skin, so much so that Bob began to perspire. "Are you cold or hot?" she asked.

Bob wiped the sweat off his brow. "How can you change the temperature?"

"Through desire. You do something similar with your mind. Imagine yourself a poor man; you become poor. Imagine yourself abundant; you radiate wealth. When you picture images in your mind and replay them with intense feelings accompanied by your senses, you make them seem real."

"Now that is folly. I can do no such thing. As a Spirit, you have more powers than I—that is, if any of this is real."

"If you want to talk about what is real, let me tell you this," said Angelica leaning closer. "The light of Christmas dwells within. When asleep, you do not remember you are but a child of God. When awake, you birth the Spirit of Christmas. Its light guides your way."

"Growing up, I barely saw the light of day, working and living in the warehouse. My life held only darkness and despair."

"The light was always there. To see it, you must release the past."

Bob glanced at the unfolding scene at Warren's Blacking Warehouse where the evil Uriah Quilp was beating other lads. He shook his head. "Impossible."

"Oh, it *is* possible," said Angelica calmly.

"How?"

"Forgiveness."

Bob pointed at Uriah Quilp. "I cannot forgive that man and all his evil. Nor can I forgive my father."

"Forgiveness is not about condoning their action. Uriah and your father are long gone, yet the pain lives in your heart. Forgiveness asks you to release your mind from the prison that ensnares you. You cannot heal unless you change what is in your heart."

"My father forced me to work for Uriah and caused my dear mother to die in a poorhouse. I will never forgive him for that."

"Then let us leave." She offered Bob the green holly once more.

Grateful to leave the scene, he grabbed the branch and was transported to an icy alleyway. There, he saw an emaciated eleven-year-old boy shivering in an alleyway, rummaging in a garbage tin.

Beating rats away with a small wooden club, the boy locates a fragment of crusty bread covered in green mold. He scrapes away the mold and devours it. He then goes back to scavenging for something else to eat.

Pointing the branch at the boy, she said, "Your father survived by his own wits on the streets of

London. His only thought was to stay alive. And that he did when he was overtaken by liquid spirits. He drank to forget the pain. And like you, he forgot his connection to the inner light and walked in darkness. That is what you saw."

Bob stared at the image of the boy in rags, fighting the rats for food. "He always told me I had an easier life. When I was his age, I was beaten, but I did have a roof over my head and food to eat. I see that he had neither."

"Compassion alters the perception of the past. Join me in blessing your father."

Bob blinked at the apparition. "Bless him?"

Angelica smiled. "Why yes. Surely, you wouldn't deprive him of a Christmas blessing."

Bob gazed at the skinny boy scouring through a garbage bin with rotten food. "I don't know what good a blessing will do. He is a lost soul."

"Not lost. He's a boy who stopped remembering." The Spirit raised a hand and faced her palm towards the boy. "In the Spirit of Christmas, I bless you."

The boy in the alleyway stops and warily glances around. "Who's there?" he whispers.

"You see," said Angelica. "He heard the blessing." She smiled at Bob. "Now you."

Asked to do what he thought was unthinkable, he vigorously shook his head.

She tapped him on the head with the green holly. "Did you not ask Scrooge to be more charitable with

Mrs. Dibble? Can you not do what you, yourself, suggested?"

Feeling rather foolish, Bob sighed, then rushed through the words, "In the Spirit of Christmas, I bless you."

"That's the best you can do?" she scoffed. "Bless him again, this time with love from your heart."

Loving his father seemed too much to ask but gazing at the boy wearing torn scraps of clothes reminded him of when he, himself, was young. Feeling some compassion, Bob said, "Bless you, Father. May you rest in peace."

The boy stumbles against the bin as if struck by lightning. He clutches his heart. Tears flow from his eyes. He remembers the light.

Bob touched his own heart. A wave of warmth spread through his body.

"A prayer of forgiveness changes the past." Angelica smiled as she extended the branch of holly. "Come, there is more to see."

When Bob clutched the rod, he found himself in a bedroom next to a midwife tending his wife, Emily.

She beams at her husband holding their firstborn. "Oh, Bob," she tells him. "What a glorious day to have a son. We shall call him Peter. Once we get back on our feet, he will grow up to be a fine lad. He can help ye start a business, like ye always wanted."

Bob swells with pride. "Yes, we will build a business together." He strokes the head of the little baby. "I promise you, Peter, you will have a great future."

He hugs his wife. "As soon as we pay off our bills, I will leave Mr. Scrooge and start anew."

Emily strokes her husband's face. "Ye are a good and gentle man, Bob Cratchit. Whatever ye do, I'll be there at yer side."

Bob stared at his wife. "Emily encouraged me and kept my hopes alive," he told the apparition. "Yet with each child, I moved further into debt. Feeding six children took me away from my dream of creating a business. I had plans, but I gave up on them." He sighed, "I ended up following my father's advice."

"Fear took over your heart," nodded Angelica.

"But what was I to do?" asked Bob. "I had responsibilities. And even then, I failed to meet them."

"Your only failure was that you forgot the light that forever glows in your heart. Your future was created from darkness, not the light."

As the tall woman spoke, light expanded from her heart creating the image of angel wings protruding from her shoulders. "We have one more visit." She extended the branch.

When Bob grabbed it, he emerged from a fog into a doctor's office. He immediately recognized the scene that had occurred a few years earlier. He could never forget it.

"Your son suffers from many maladies including rickets," says the man dressed in a black coat.

"Is there any hope for Tiny Tim?"

The doctor shrugs. "Many children suffer from such maladies. With better food, medicines, sunshine, and fresh air, your son would have a better chance of surviving."

"But I can hardly afford bread and potatoes."

"London's winter does his lungs no good," says the doctor shaking his head. He opens the door to his office. "I wish there was more I could tell you."

"That visit brought misery," lamented Bob, tears streaming down his face. "Why show me this?"

"To free you," said the apparition, emanating the scent of fresh pine. Her face glowed. "You must let go of the walls of ice surrounding your heart. Only then can you choose the light of love and return Home. When you free the past, you welcome the present."

She raised the branch and offered it one more time. "Another Spirit will show you the way."

Grabbing hold, Bob was whisked back to his tiny office. He glanced around the depressing counting house. The familiarity of his surroundings brought momentary comfort from his miserable memories. He sought to ask Angelica a question, but she faded from his eyes, leaving nothing but the memory of her smiling face, the flowing red dress with evergreen garlands, the tinkling bells in her hair, and the scent of pine.

He sighed, believing the whole episode to be nothing more than a hallucination from overwork. He glanced at the pile of papers on his desk and released a bigger sigh. Another long night on Christmas Eve. He lifted his quill above the ledger but could not concentrate. Overwhelmed with fatigue, he rested his weary head on the desk and soon fell fast asleep.

Chapter Three
The Second Spirit

Ding, dong. Ding, dong. Ding…

The clock on Scrooge's wall struck eight, startling Bob from his slumber. A draft of wind blew through the air, causing the candle flame to flicker. He shook his head to clear his thoughts. When he saw Scrooge's office ablaze with light, he became frightened that his employer had somehow returned. He timidly peered through the doorway.

His mouth fell open at the sight of a buxom, olive-skinned woman dressed in a luxurious green velvet robe with the collar and sleeves trimmed in white fur. Wearing a wreath of holly over her curly brown hair, she stood in bare feet surrounded by brightly colored packages with sparkly ribbons and bows. Sumptuous cakes and puddings, fruits and steaming chestnuts, and an assortment of savory delicacies littered Scrooge's desk.

Bob walked warily into Scrooge's office. "Wh-who are you?"

The woman's eyes sparkled as she gazed at Bob. The jolly figure laughed so heartily her entire body shook with merriment. "You do not know me?"

"Are you the Spirit of Christmas Present?" he asked, approaching the warmth of the blazing fire and the angelic form.

The bawdy Spirit chuckled. "Call me Noella, my dear." Her eyes twinkled with mischief. "I'm here to steal you away from your dreary office and into the joyous Presence of Christmas?"

"Do I have a choice?"

Another hearty laugh escaped from the apparition's generous mouth. "Of course. You can come willingly, or you can come unwillingly." She held her jiggling belly while she continued to laugh. "The choice is yours!"

"Then let's be done with this," sighed Bob.

She giggled. "You choose wisely, my dear."

When the robust woman clutched his hand, Bob detected the smell of yummy gingerbread. Inhaling the fragrance, he was transported through a mist to a festive party. People were dressed in fine evening garments, eating tasty hors d'oeuvres. Remaining invisible, Bob and Noella approached Scrooge's nephew standing near the fireplace.

Fred sips a glass of brandy as he listens to a well-dressed man with saggy jowls.

"Scrooge is the main lender in town," groans Albert Bell. "The miser holds us to ransom."

"I know you despise my uncle," says Fred. "Surely, he has his faults."

"Faults! The heartless scoundrel gave nothing but scowls and a piece of coal when asked to help

feed the children. He would squeeze blood from a corpse as payment for debts owed. No doubt the swindler alters the books."

Fred raises his hand in protest. "As long as Bob Cratchit oversees the ledgers, everything is in order. He's an honest and honorable man."

"That helps us little when we are gouged by your uncle. We need someone who offers honest rates."

The conversation between the two men continued as Noella nodded to Bob. "There are many who respect you."

"It does little good to feed my family," responded Bob.

"My dear, you could serve your family better if you respected yourself."

Bob squinted at the Spirit. "Why say this? I respect myself well enough."

"Ah, respect, you say," snickered Noella. "What about your dreams and desires? If you respected them, you would be living a different life."

"What do you mean?"

Noella waved her hand at the festive gathering. "These people desired a Christmas celebration. Without that desire, they would not be here."

"I desire to be at home with my family. That will be satisfied later," countered Bob.

Noella laughed, causing her body to shake again. "Later? What about now? I've come to remind you of Christmas Present."

"I celebrate Christmas every year."

"Ah, but you neglect the Spirit of Christmas the other days."

"Scrooge makes it impossible to celebrate more than once a year."

"Restore yourself, my dear, and think not of Scrooge but only of the present. That is where your power resides. When you live in the present, you receive miraculous gifts."

The jolly woman moved towards the well-dressed man complaining about Scrooge. She rubbed her hands together then placed them over his head. A shower of green glitter poured from her hands along with an aroma of gingerbread. The demeanor on his face immediately shifted as if he had consumed a glass of fine punch.

Smiling, Albert Bell pats Fred on the shoulder. "As long as Bob Cratchit works for Scrooge, the ledgers will be correct. If he ran the business, we would all be better off. But let us enjoy the evening and celebrate Christmas."

Fred smiles at his friend's change of heart. "That's the spirit!"

Albert calls out to the crowd, "Let us sing a carol."

Fred leads everyone to the piano where his wife positions herself on a chair near the keyboard. She begins to play.

The group joins in song. "The First Noel, the Angels did say…"

"My favorite carol," chuckled Noella. "Know well that one joyous feeling alters the present."

Amazed by Albert Bell's change of demeanor, Bob remarked, "As one from the Spirit world, you can do many things."

Noella pulled on his ears. "Did you not listen to Angelica and learn from the past? The Spirit of Christmas resides in you, just like me."

Staring at her bare feet, Bob noticed for the first time that each toe was encircled by a golden ring. "You have magical powers I do not have."

She released a jolly laugh. "You desire joy, do you not?"

"Of course."

She swept her arm in the green velvet sleeve over the room. "And what about the finer things in life like these other people?"

"Those are for the wealthy. I am just a poor man."

"Ah, so noble, my dear. Seeing yourself as a *poor man* merely demonstrates your lack of respect for yourself. Do you not desire an easier life?"

"Yes, but that is beyond my means."

"It is beyond your means because you sleep through the present."

Bob scratched his head. "I may be sleepwalking while with you, but I assure you I am very much awake during the day."

Noella put her arm around Bob. He inhaled gingerbread while she whispered in his ear. "Answer this question, my dear. What do you desire now?"

Bob scanned the festive scene with merrymakers dressed in their finery, eating, drinking, and laughing with one another. "I desire the end of growing debts so I can provide proper medical treatment for Tiny Tim."

"And?"

"Ample food for my family."

"And?"

"That would be plenty, for it would bring me great joy."

"Spoken by someone with little Christmas Spirit. Come, my dear," grinned Noella. "Imagine your wildest dreams. What would you truly desire?"

He glanced at the sumptuous food on the table, the crystal chandelier hanging from the ceiling, and Fred's wife playing "The First Noel" on the piano. "How miraculous it would be if I had the financial means to live like them."

"Yes," encouraged Noella. "Respect what you desire. Broaden your vision."

A guilty look flashed across his face. "I would wish for a large home for my family — with bedrooms for each of my children and one for me and my wife. And a business where my children and I worked together." His eyes sparkled as if handed a glittering present. "Most importantly, I wish Tiny Tim would be cured and live a long, happy life."

Bob nodded with satisfaction. "Yes, that would make me very happy."

The apparition clapped her hands, sending a shower of green sparkles in the air. "Now you're desiring, my dear. With practice, you can receive miraculous presents. For every day is Christmas!"

She signaled Bob to grab her hand. "Come, my dear. There is more to see."

The two were whisked from the stately home into an old, wooden house where an elderly couple quivered before the miserly lender.

"A few more days, Mr. Scrooge," begs the wife. "It's Christmas."

"Bah! Humbug! You have not paid another month." He scans the bare room with a few sticks of broken furniture. "I don't need another flea-bitten shack." His eyes settle on the wife's wedding band. He jabs a finger at the thin silver ring. "I'll take that for last month's payment." He then stabs the finger at the husband's hand. "And I'll take yours for this month's payment."

"'Twas… my father's!" cried the husband.

The woman gasps. "Our rings? Surely, ye don't mean that, Mr. Scrooge."

"Are you deaf? Off with the rings – or lose your shack."

The woman's husband chokes back tears. He nods for his wife to remove her ring.

"I don't have all night," berates Scrooge.

Tears trickle down her cheeks as the woman twists the silver band off her finger. She kisses it, then drops it into her husband's palm. He removes his ring and hands the two wedding bands to the scowling lender.

Scrooge gleefully pockets the rings and reaches for the doorknob. Before leaving, he tells

the weeping couple, "I shan't be so lenient next
month should you not have the next installment."
He leaves the couple in tears.

Bob whispered to the Spirit, "Scrooge is despicable. Can you not sprinkle some of your magic dust on him?"

"I dare not interfere. He will soon have other-worldly visitors."

"Will you be one of the Spirits?"

She shook her head, causing the curls of brown hair to jiggle. "Each person gets special visitors. Your mother's love beckoned womanly Spirits to awaken you and remind you that love is ever-present."

Staring at the weeping couple, Bob sighed, "Not to Mr. Scrooge."

"Ah, he holds financial power over many, whereas you have compassion. Still, you live in fear, my dear, and feel powerless to pay your debts."

"That does not seem fair, Spirit."

"Fair is what you make of it." She grabbed Bob's hand. "There's more to see."

She whisked him to a familiar dwelling, his tiny four-room house.

Wearing metal braces on his legs, Tiny Tim winces
with pain. He leans on his crutches as he helps his
siblings, Lucy and Matthew, decorate a spindly tree
with paper ornaments. His oldest brother, Peter,
wearing one of Bob's old shirts with an oversize
collar, hangs six worn stockings near the fireplace
and plops an apple and a chestnut into each.

In the kitchen, Bob's wife bustles around the stove. With an apron over her worn Christmas gown spruced up with red ribbons, Emily stirs a pot of boiling potatoes. Near her, one of the daughters, Belinda, pours a cup of flour into a bowl containing ingredients for a Christmas pudding.

"Will Father be late again?" she asks.

Her mother sighs. "I expect so. Yer father's such a good man. But I so fret for him. He puts on a brave face, yet he carries far too many burdens. We've fallen behind on our bills, and we have no money for doctors."

"I can ask if Mrs. Jingle needs another maid," says Belinda.

Wiping her eyes, Emily Cratchit hugs her daughter. "Yer already washing clothes for Mrs. Bell. Yer father feels bad that ye and yer sister pay some of our bills.

"I'm glad to help, Mother," says Belinda. "Father loves us, and he adores you."

"And I love him." She hesitates before speaking. "But I can no longer brighten his life when he comes home from work. He fears the future. I've failed him." She turns her face to hide the tears trickling down her cheek.

Grabbing Noella's green velvet robe, Bob pleaded, "Don't make my wife suffer. She deserves better. My family deserves better."

The apparition patted Bob's arm. "My dear, you and your family do deserve better. But you must awaken from a deep sleep and find the bright star that heralds the Child who has been born. The shining beacon births you to the presence of love where you can vision a renewed life. But you must have faith and learn to trust."

"Trust who?"

"Have you not been paying attention, my dear?" She tugged on his ear. "The Spirit of Christmas, of course. Believe and be open to guidance."

"How do I do this?"

"You ask the obvious," chuckled Noella. "Stay awake; keep your eyes open. See the signs. When you hear the sound of church bells, let them remind you that the guiding power of Spirit beckons you to your true Home where love and inner peace abide. See everyone as part of the Christmas pageant to bring you *Home*. Even Ebenezer."

Bob's mouth dropped open. "Mr. Scrooge? How can that be?"

Noella laughed, causing her tummy to jiggle. "He who has forgotten about love is most in need of it. You teach him about love by living it yourself."

"But I do love my family," protested Bob.

"Ah, love you give them, but you are stingy, like Ebenezer, about showering love on yourself. Have you not heard about loving your neighbor as yourself?" Noella clapped her hands, producing a shower of green sparkles. "When you feel loved, you have so much more to give to the world. And since your very essence is love, you have plenty to give. Be a living candle and light darkened rooms in the Spirit of Christmas."

The angelic figure poked him in the stomach and laughed heartily. "Do you not love your wife?"

Bob blushed. "Of course, I do."

"Can you direct some of that love to Ebenezer?"

Horrified at that prospect, Bob shook his head. "I cannot. I despise the man. He loves money, not people."

"All the more reason to look upon him and see him through the eyes of love."

Unable to comprehend her words, Bob shook his head again. "You ask the impossible. He is a miserable old soul."

"You see only his body. Look upon Ebenezer and see beyond his physical form. Know him as your teacher."

"Heaven forbid," said Bob, shaking his head violently. "His god is greed."

Noella chuckled. "Ah, but he shows you a tortured soul who desperately needs loving kindness. Surely, you could spare a few ounces of compassion?"

"I loathe him more than I pity him."

"Look at me," said the Spirit, peering into his eyes. "I want you to know what love is, and I'm here to show you. I want you to feel love with your senses, to listen with ears of love, and to see through the eyes of love. Look at me."

Doing as instructed, he gazed into Noella's green eyes. He inhaled a trace of sweet buttery gingerbread. Warmth rushed through his body.

"Breathe in love," she commanded. "Yes, breathe in the fragrant essence of love."

Bob filled his lungs with warm air. It entered his body, relaxing his muscles, causing a wave of peace and calm. His senses expanded. A whiff of Noella's gingerbread merged into the aroma of plum pudding coming from the kitchen of his tiny house. The fragrances circled up his nose and exploded into an array of savory spices—cinnamon, clove, and nutmeg. His mouth watered as he imagined tasting the pudding steaming in a pot. His hearing and sight became magnified as he watched Tiny Tim and the other children decorate the tree, talking about the Christmas goose. And when his wife whispered to their daughter, Belinda, about her love for Bob, his skin tingled.

"Don't resist. Embrace every experience with love."

A rush of emotions swirled inside, each like a different fragrance. Sadness shifted to compassion; fear morphed into love. Each emotion dissolved into the joy of being alive.

"Expand your mind; open your heart." Noella placed her hand on his chest, igniting green sparks.

Bob jumped as if touched by an electric probe.

"Fear not," she chuckled. "Let the love in. Feel the love you hold for your family. Instill that kind of love into whatever you desire. And if anguish and pain from the past blot out desire, bless those feelings with love so they may dissolve. That is the only way to find your way Home where Christmas is celebrated every day."

Basking in a warm glow, he closed his eyes. Intense heat radiated in his heart, opening it like a clam shell. Immersed in an iridescent green bubble of love, Bob felt an incredible sense of wellbeing. He breathed in love, circulating it through his bloodstream, immersing his body, releasing fear, anger, and shame. He felt cared for and loved without a worry. Euphoria and awe filled him as if he had consumed several glasses of Christmas punch.

"Love is timeless," crooned Noella. "It dissolves separation, for there is no room for separation with love. Love is ever-present, all consuming, revealing Divine Presence."

The angelic apparition touched Bob's forehead. "See through the eyes of love. You are a holy child of God, like everyone. Imagine Ebenezer. He has forgotten he is also a child of God. He desperately needs love. Give voice to that love."

Consumed with rapture, Bob spoke without a moment's hesitation. "Bless you, Mr. Scrooge. May you feel love in your heart. I bless you with the joy of Christmas."

After a timeless moment, Noella chuckled. "That wasn't so hard. Was it, my dear?" She removed her finger from his forehead. "How do you feel?"

Bob blinked his eyes open as if coming out of a trance. He touched his chest. "I feel sorry for Mr. Scrooge. I have a wife and six children. He has no one."

"Ah. See how you opened your mind and heart, my dear? Doing so changed the outside world. As you come to know love, you discover the unity of all things. When you place your attention there, you become present with the Divine."

He was about to answer when he spotted movement under Noella's velvet green robe. He pointed at an exposed naked leg next to her bare feet. "What are you keeping there?"

"Ah, a final lesson for you, my dear man." She opened the bottom of her robe and revealed two children clinging to the garment. A young girl blinked her eyes as if in a stupor while a young boy cowered, terrified of the light.

"These children represent ignorance and fear. They are here to remind you that when you believe the negative thoughts and ideas handed down by family, teachers, and ministers and adopt them as true, you will fear leaving them behind. Unless you break those rusting chains of ignorance and fear, you are destined to repeat the past."

She closed the robe around the children. "Do not forget that you are a child of God. Your true purpose is to act like a beacon and love fearlessly. Shine your light and help others break free from the fog of terror so they can see their oneness with the Divine."

"You ask much of me," said Bob. "I am but a simple man."

"Ah," smiled Noella. "Blessed are the meek for they shall inherit the world. Surrender to the Holy Presence of Christmas and embrace your essence — love. Remember, my dear, forgiveness allows you to let love flow."

Placing her hand on his heart, Noella pronounced, "Forgive yourself, Bob Cratchit, and let the love flow *to* you. Doing so removes that which stops love from filling your heart. Become like an overflowing well. Pour love to those who need it, especially the igno-rant and fearful. Ebenezer is one such soul. He needs Christmas more than anyone else."

Pondering her words, he never considered that his employer had a soul, let alone one that housed love. In the past, Bob's fear prevented him from feel-ing compassion for his employer.

"Whenever you encounter ignorance or fear, use the light of knowledge and the elixir of love." She held out her hand to Bob. "Come, my dear. My time with you is almost over. The future awaits you."

Bob pointed towards his wife bustling around the stove. "Can I not stay here longer?"

"You will meet your family soon enough. Come."

With a heavy heart, Bob grabbed her hand and was transported back to his desk. There the candle flickered with a gust of wind.

Chapter Four
The Third Spirit

*D*ing, dong. Ding, dong. Ding…

When the wall clock in Scrooge's office struck nine, Bob rubbed his eyes. Noella with her luxurious green velvet robe and white trimmed collar and sleeves was gone. In her place stood a purple-robed figure holding a torch in the right hand. The face was shrouded by a purple hood.

Feeling faint, Scrooge's clerk steadied himself against the desk. "Are y-you the Spirit of Christmas Future?"

The figure waved the torch at Bob. Smoke the color of lavender rose like a finger signaling him to follow. "My frankincense will lift you to the future. Come."

Not wanting to face the future, Bob blurted, "Do I have a choice?"

The hooded head nodded. "You can choose to come willingly or unwillingly. The choice is yours." She waved the torch again.

Inhaling the warm, sweet, woody fragrance with added notes of citrus and spice, Bob felt as if he was entering a church. He timidly stepped forward into a twirling vortex. His body began to spin in a clockwise fashion. Coming to a dizzying stop, he collapsed on a polished wooden floor. Rising, he steadied himself and found himself in a stately residence. His mouth dropped open at the sight of a huge Christmas tree. Decorated with red and green baubles and silver tinsel, it graced the corner of an immense, well-lit drawing room complete with a grand piano. The man of simple tastes marveled at the roaring fire in the fireplace, the lavish furnishings, and the paintings of angels hanging on the walls.

"Where am I?" asked Bob.

The purple-robed figure removed the hood, revealing a petite Asian woman. Straight, shoulder-length, violet hair dangled from the left side of her head while the hair on her right side was cut short, not touching her ear.

Bob faltered as he stared at the Spirit. "Wh-who are you?"

The woman stroked her violet hair. "I am Uriella." Her right hand lifted the blazing torch. Wisps of frankincense curled towards the ceiling. "I light the way of What May Be."

No sooner had the angelic figure spoken when children ran into the room followed by their mother.

"Father comes home soon," cries the eldest boy, dressed in a neatly pressed brown suit and shirt.

"Peter, you look so handsome," beams his mother decked out in a flowing red silk dress. "Come, children," she says, "Let us practice those carols once more before your father arrives."

Five children gather around the piano while a sixth, Belinda, plays the ivory keys.

The mother leads them in singing, "Joy to the World…"

Remaining invisible, Bob listened to their vibrant voices. Tears streamed down his face. "How can that be?" he asked the Spirit. "Has my wife married another man?"

"Look," replied Uriella. "He arrives home now."

Bob stared at a well-dressed man tiptoeing into the room so as not to disturb the singing. He barely recognized himself in such splendid attire.

Not noticing the approaching man, the family continues to sing, "…And heaven and nature sing, and heaven and nature sing…"

"Father," cries Tiny Tim, spotting his father. Without crutches or metal braces, he runs to meet him, followed by the other children and his wife. They surround him with hugs and kisses.

Gawking at the scene, Bob stuttered, "H-how can that be? Tiny Tim, the house, the splendor?"

Uriella pointed to her torch. "The future is lit by the fire of your heart's desires. When you listen to your heart and choose from that place of desire, the future responds. When you neglect the wishes of your heart, the future responds accordingly."

"Are you telling me I can create a future such as this?"

The petite Asian woman waved her torch at the lavish scene. "This is but one of many versions of the future. Your life is what your thoughts make it. What you experience in your tomorrows is the result of what you think today. You have countless choices."

"But how do I choose?"

"Let your heart be your guide."

Bob gazed at his children. Tiny Tim had never looked so healthy.

"But what about my son? How did he get better?"

"You had the means to provide doctors and medicines."

His wide eyes wandered over the splendid room and the festive setting. "And I can have all this?" he asked in a disbelieving voice.

"More, if you so desire. Remember, you are a child of God meant to bring joy to the world."

"Please tell me, Spirit of the Future, what must I do?

"Connect with your heart and use your mind to create your future. Every day you have limitless choices. Think poverty; that is what you shall have. Think abundance, and it shall come."

"You make it sound so simple."

Uriella lifted the long violet hair on the left side of her face. "Do you like my hair this way?"

Not wanting to offend the Spirit, he merely said, "It's... unusual."

She waved her torch and her face transformed. The short hair now appeared on the left side of her head while the long, straight violet hair hung on the right. "What about now?"

Bob rubbed his eyes. "How did you do that?"

Uriella smiled. "I desired a different look, so I chose another thought." She waved the torch and her hair returned to the way it had been. Stroking the long hair, she announced, "I like it better this way." She then pointed at Bob's hair. "Would you like another style?"

Placing his hands on his muttonchop sideburns, he shook his head vigorously. "I shall keep what I have, thank you."

"And so it shall be."

Scratching his head, he asked, "Can I really choose whatever I desire?"

"Do you not realize you have free will?"

Bob waved his hand at the stately residence. "I do not feel free to will such luxury."

"That's because you have chained your mind to tiny thoughts."

"I don't understand."

Uriella gazed at her torch and inhaled the frankincense. "Most humans have forgotten they are spiritual beings on a blessed journey on Earth. Each has chosen a vessel that offers unique experiences. Imagine every living being as a clay pot. Inside each pot grows a plant. Some emerge as roses, others as carnations." She eyed the color of her torch's smoke. "I, myself, prefer lavender. But those who grow weeds do so freely because they wish to experience weediness."

"I still don't understand," said Bob.

The apparition peered intently at the man in front of her. "You, for one, have chosen a pot that sprouts poverty."

"I didn't choose that," protested Bob. "I was a victim of circumstances."

"I was waiting for the word *victim* to appear," said Uriella. "You are merely the victim of the seeds you have planted in your mind. When you cultivate the same tiny seeds of unworthiness and fear, you grow the same plants in your earthen pot."

Uriella placed her torch above Bob's head. "I am here to radiate the soil in your vessel so you realize the power you hold over your life. With the power of choice, you can choose the bright flowers of forgiveness and love to bloom in your heart. That is the Spirit of Christmas. And that Spirit will show you where to go, what to do, whom to meet, and what to say. When you share your bouquet with others, you help them remember to return Home to the eternal Christmas."

She brought the torch in front of her face, casting a shadow over Bob. "Forget about love, and your future will be like others who stumble in darkness. To help you choose wisely, I must show you another future where the light has been hidden."

The Asian woman blew into the torch, sending a puff of frankincense into the air. The scene vanished, and Bob twirled forward in a circular fashion. With his head pounding, he collapsed on a scratched wooden floor. Instead of a well-lit room, Bob found himself in Scrooge's office. His employer was hunched over his desk, an older man with a meaner look on his face, counting coins.

Scrooge glances up and scowls at a young man with scraggly long hair standing before him. "So, you want to work as my new clerk?"

"Yes, sir," responds the eager man.

"Good. I was tired of paying Cratchit for work that was never complete. You won't give me any trouble about working on Christmas, will you?"

"No, sir."

Scrooge nods and grins, revealing a missing front tooth. "And you agree to start at ten shillings a week?"

"Yes, sir." He clears his throat. "I'm sure you will be inclined to reward me with an increase — at the appropriate time."

Scrooge eyes the scraggly hair. "We shall see." He hands the new clerk a ledger. "Cratchit was slow but efficient. See that you are efficient AND quick. Record these new receipts."

The young man takes the pile of papers and bows. "Gladly, sir."

He walks to Bob Cratchit's old desk and picks up a quill. Dipping it in the inkwell, he works on the ledger. He peers at his new employer from the corner of his eye, watching Scrooge bag the coins from his desk and deposit them in a drawer, whereupon he locks it and stores the key in his pocket.

Bob faced Uriella. "Tell me, oh Spirit. Was I let go by Mr. Scrooge?"

The purple-robed woman responded by waving the fiery torch. As frankincense snaked upward, she and Bob were propelled outside the office where time had moved forward.

In the swirling snow, Scrooge hobbles down a side street and clutches his coat tight around his body. A hooded man jumps from the shadows and accosts him. Before Scrooge could scream, the man stabs the miser in the back. He searches the fallen body and retrieves a key from the pocket. No one hears the bleeding man's muffled cries. Left in the gutter, Scrooge exhales his last breath.

Horrified, Bob cried, "That was the new clerk, wasn't it?"

Uriella nodded.

"What happened to me?"

The Spirit replied by blowing into the torch causing a huge puff of smoke plunging Bob back into the twirling vortex. When the haze cleared, he came to a halt.

Tombstones appear in a snow-covered cemetery, the paupers' section.

"No," screamed Bob. "Not here."

The Asian woman glided across the frigid ground and stopped before a gravesite.

Terrified at what he might see, Bob warily approached a tombstone. He gasped. Tiny Tim never reached his teens. The grieving father buried his face in his hands and wept.

"No!" he sobbed. "The pain is too great. Take me away."

Uriella lowered the flickering torch near the grave next to his son. Bob raised his head, then wailed uncontrollably. The date of his own death was a mere two months after the passing of Tiny Tim.

"I left my wife and children without support—just like my father."

His knees sank to the snow. "Oh, Spirit," cried Bob. "I can't bear a future like this. Tell me, if I embrace Christmas Spirit, can I change the future? And if there be such things as miracles, I will believe in them."

Uriella stood still, holding the fiery torch. It radiated light as snow swirled across the graves.

Bob sobbed, "I can change. I must change. I will awaken and learn from the past. I will listen to my heart's desires and live in the present with love in my heart—for everyone including Mr. Scrooge. I will choose wisely and fulfill my dreams and change this horrid future. Tiny Tim must live!"

The purple-robed figure placed a hand on Bob's shoulder and squeezed.

Bob shut his eyes to that horrible future and pleaded, "Please, anything but this." He felt a jolt to his shoulders.

"Get up. GET UP!" shouted a voice.

"I promise I'll change."

"Wake up, you crazy fool."

Bob's eyes popped open. Before him stood Scrooge, his eyes blazing with fury. Bob frantically looked around for Uriella. There was no sign of her.

"You've fallen asleep, you lazy oaf," shouted Scrooge. He shook his clerk's shoulder. "I'll not pay you to sleep on my time. Just as well I checked on you." He glanced at the stack of papers and open ledger. "You must come back tomorrow and work on Christmas!"

Bob's hand reached for his own face. He pinched his cheek. "Ouch!" He patted his legs and his arms. "I'm alive!"

He gazed at Scrooge as if for the first time. "'Tis you, Ebenezer, isn't it?"

Scrooge winced at being addressed by his first name. "You impudent fool. Have you been drinking?"

Bob jumped to his feet. The future could be changed! He was sure of it. He would let go of the past, open his heart to the presence of Christmas, and use his mind to create a healthy, prosperous future for his family. He would believe in miracles. Noticing his scowling employer, he wrapped his arms around him in a bear hug.

Startled, Scrooge struggled to push him away. "I'll not have any of that. Have you lost your senses, Cratchit?"

Bob laughed hysterically. "No, Ebenezer. But thank you, thank you! I have come to my senses." Giddy, he moved to hug his employer again but was immediately rebuffed by protesting arms.

"What spirits have you been drinking?" shouted the enraged miser.

"I have not been drinking, but I've had plenty of Spirits." He chuckled. "I assure you, I'm of sound mind, maybe for the first time in my life. But there's no time to waste."

"Now you're making sense! I'll not have you waste my time. I'll see you here tomorrow, Christmas Day!"

Bob stopped laughing. "No, Ebenezer," he said, now quite serious. "I'll be with my family on Christmas. From now on, I celebrate Christmas every day. I daresay you should also."

Scrooge reacted as if hit with an anvil. "Christmas every day? Bah! Humbug! You must be mad!"

"For the first time, Ebenezer, I am madly in love with life."

"Go home, you fool. Sleep it off. When you have come to your senses, return here tomorrow. Or else find yourself another job."

Bob felt a twinge of fear in his heart. A flurry of worries swirled in his mind. If he was out of work, how would he pay off his debts or provide treatment for Tiny Tim? He cringed at the image of the tombstones.

"Are you listening?" barked Scrooge.

That question broke Bob's train of thought. *Is this a test from Spirits?* he wondered.

Closing his eyes, he imagined the scent of pine and Christmas Past murmuring, "Let go of what no longer serves you."

He no longer wanted to be bullied by a tyrant. The Spirit of Christmas Future told him that every choice shaped his tomorrows. If he submitted to fear, he would continue an impoverished life. If he took the risk and listened to his heart's desire, he would receive guidance on what to do, where to go, whom to talk to, and what to say.

The image of the stately residence popped into his mind. He recalled the drawing room and the huge Christmas tree with red and green baubles and silver tinsel. He remembered the grand fireplace with a roaring fire and the ornate paintings of angels adorning the walls.

He flashed to the Spirit of Christmas Present and remembered her instruction to breathe in love. Placing his hand on his heart, he filled his lungs with the breath of love. A rush of warm air entered his body, relaxing his muscles, calming his nerves. His senses expanded. He heard the wheezing of Scrooge's breath and smelt the pork pie he must've eaten over dinner. He spotted twitching muscles on his employer's cheeks indicating nervousness and fear.

He recalled the buttery smell of gingerbread and heard Noella's faint whisper: "Don't resist. Expand your mind; open your heart."

Bob pressed his hand against his heart where a burning sensation intensified, melting anxiety and fear. Overcome with the rush of emotions, he imagined a golden bubble of love surrounding him. All he had to do was remember that love was ever-present.

Still holding his hand against his chest, he breathed in love, circulating it through his body. Fear shifted to a feeling of elation. He opened his eyes and faced Scrooge who looked as if he had seen a terrible ghost. What he actually saw and felt was the warm glow radiating from Bob. For Scrooge, that seemed like madness.

Remembering what Noella had told him, Bob smiled. "Ebenezer. 'Tis not too late to change."

Stepping away from his clerk to ward off another hug, Scrooge winced. "What madness are you saying?"

"I have witnessed your death and faced my own. I no longer want to live in fear. I have listened to the voices of Christmas and beseech you to do the same. There is only love."

"You oaf," scoffed Scrooge. "You *have* lost your mind."

Bob chuckled. "I've come to my senses, Ebenezer. I will create a business that helps those in need and treats them with love and respect."

Scrooge gagged as if swallowing repulsive medicine. "Love and respect? There's no money in that!"

"I beg your pardon. That is the only way to make money."

Bob walked towards the coat rack and grabbed his hat and scarf. "I wish you a merry Christmas, Ebenezer." He reached for the door.

"I expect you here tomorrow to finish your work!" shouted Scrooge.

Turning around, Bob faced the scowling man. "Continue your ways and you will die an old, wretched man, friendless and unloved."

Bob gently hugged Scrooge, who stood frozen this time, mouth open in disbelief at the audacity of his clerk. He quickly regained his composure and pushed Bob towards the door.

"You *are* crazy. And fired. When you come crawling back tomorrow, I'll cut your wages in half. Do you hear?!"

Bemused by Scrooge's bluster, Bob said, "Your threats mean nothing today, Ebenezer. I'll take no more abuse." He pointed at the candle. "The light is ever-present. Be prepared for visitors later. I daresay, the first will be Jacob Marley."

"Jacob? You *are* mad."

"Listen to the Spirits. Merry Christmas."

"Bah! Humbug!"

Bob brushed his coat as if shedding off burdens. He smiled at his soon-to-be ex-employer and walked out unchained from the past. He felt light, even giddy, as if a sack of rocks had been lifted from his shoulder. Feeling like a schoolboy, he skidded along the icy path, laughing at the sheer lunacy of standing up to Scrooge the day before Christmas. Maybe, it was not too late to start a business.

When the church bells began tolling, Bob paused. Others may think him mad, but he had been crazy all these years, not standing up to Scrooge. When the final bell struck ten, Bob skidded to a halt. As it so happened, he had stopped in front of the home of Scrooge's nephew. The lights were ablaze in the house. The sound of a piano with Christmas carols being sung meant a party was underway.

Knock on the door, beckoned the voice whispering inside Bob's head. In the past, he would have brushed off the message, but today he knew it came from the Spirit of Christmas Present. Approaching the door, he rapped on it. When a maid answered, he asked to speak with the nephew.

"Do you have an invitation?" she asked.

"No, my good woman," answered Bob, chuckling at his own folly. "Who needs an invitation to wish someone a merry Christmas?"

The maid hesitated, but when she saw Bob's twinkling eyes, she told him to wait. Standing by the door, he rubbed his hands for warmth and watched the candles flickering in the window.

In a moment, Fred appeared. His eyes widened in surprise. "Cratchit, has something happened to my uncle?"

Bob laughed. "No. Well, yes. Your uncle may need your help."

"What kind of help?" asked the nephew, his furrowed brow showing concern.

"He fired me this evening."

"He what? Why?"

Bob brushed away the question. "It matters not, sir. Your uncle is a lonely, unhappy man. He could use your company now that I am no longer in his service."

"What will you do?"

"Not quite sure, sir," answered Bob. "But I don't mean to spoil your party. I thought you should know, as you are his only relative. He needs your love."

Bob bowed to the nephew. "I must be off. May you and your wife have a merry Christmas." He waved goodbye and started to walk down the street.

"Wait," yelled Fred. "Come in for a drink. I wish to hear more."

Chapter Five
The End of It

It was after eleven when Bob burst through the door. Spotting his wife huddled near the fireplace, he rushed into her arms. He hugged and kissed her as if he had not seen her in months.

"What's got over ye, Robert?" cried his red-faced wife. She nodded at the children. "We were all worried. Ye never worked this late on Christmas Eve. That horrid Scrooge. He's a beast of a man."

"'Tis Christmas, my dear," said her husband. "Even Mr. Scrooge deserves some kindness. Besides, something marvelous has happened."

Overwhelmed with joy, Bob grabbed each child — Tiny Tim, Matthew, Lucy, Belinda, and his eldest son Peter — and smothered them in hugs until they were all giggling and laughing.

Emily smelled her husband's breath. "Have ye been drinking, Robert Cratchit? Ye seem unlike yourself."

"I've had a brandy with Mr. Scrooge's nephew," he confessed. "But it's not the alcohol that brings me such merriment, my dear." He paused and looked around. "Where's Martha?"

"She's been putting in long hours at the milliner's shop," said Emily. "After work, she planned to drop off a present for a friend. She never misses Christmas dinner."

"I hope she comes home soon. But gather 'round, everyone."

His wife and the five children gathered around him, captivated by his excitement.

"I was blessed by angels this holy day." He raised his eyes upward as if to acknowledge the angelic visitors. "I was given a true Christmas present."

"What is it?" cried Tiny Tim.

He hugged his son whose legs were supported by iron braces. "We must first visit the church as we always do on Christmas Eve. Then we shall have our splendid dinner." He sniffed the air. "The bird smells delicious."

He sent his wife a loving smile. "No doubt, you have cooked the most splendid goose with onion and sage stuffing."

"Are ye right?" asked his wife, wondering what had come over her husband. He was usually cheerful about Christmas, but this time his eyes sparkled and his body glowed.

Bob kissed his wife. "My dear, I've never been so happy to be with my family." He glanced at the clock. "But it's getting late. Today is not one to break tradition. Tiny Tim and I must visit the church before midnight like we always do and pray for his health."

"Then off with ye," said Emily, pushing him towards the door. "The children and I shall finish preparations. All shall be ready when ye return."

"And then I shall tell a miraculous story," he said with a twinkle in his eyes. "So much to tell." He chuckled, then burst into a huge belly laugh. "So much to tell!"

"Tell us now," begged Peter, wearing the oversize collar that used to belong to his father.

"The story will have to wait till Christmas—after I return." He picked up Tiny Tim's crutch. "Come, lad." He hoisted his youngest son off the ground and placed him on his shoulders.

"Hurry home," pressed his wife. She turned to the other children. "We've more preparations. Help me in the kitchen."

While the children hurried after their mother, Bob and Tiny Tim left the house and made their way to the old stone church. There, other visitors gathered to pray before the night turned into Christmas morning. Settling into a pew, father and son sat in stillness watching the candles flicker on the altar.

While Bob had visited the church many times, he'd never paid close attention to the detail on one of the stained-glass windows. It depicted three angels hovering above a glowing manger. He had always focused on the manger, but this time he couldn't help but notice the angels. They wore wings of light. He detected three scents hanging in the air—pine, gingerbread, and frankincense.

Smiling, Bob raised his eyes to the heavens and offered a silent prayer of thanks for his angelic visitors. Without them, he would be stumbling in the dark, sleepwalking through life. He vowed to listen to the holy whispers when they came and to do as bidden. He now knew that he was never alone and could always ask for guidance should he fall into fear or forgetfulness. He promised to live in the present and treat each day as Christmas.

"Father," said Tiny Tim. "I see angels."

Startled by his son's comment, he asked, "Where?"

When Tiny Tim pointed at the stained glass, Bob said, "There are three of them in the glass."

"No, they're floating above the glass. They're so bright it's hurting my eyes."

If he had not been visited by the angelic figures, he would have assumed Tiny Tim was imagining the light. But now he knew otherwise.

Bob placed his arm around his son. "Always look for the light. Angels will be there when you need them." He gently squeezed Tiny Tim's shoulder. "Let's ask them to shower our family with Christmas Spirit."

Tiny Tim nodded. "If it wasn't for Christmas, the lame wouldn't walk, and the blind couldn't see."

"Exactly!"

Father and son closed their eyes in prayer. Those in the church would later state that a glowing light surrounded the two praying in silence.

Bong. Bong. Bong.…

When the church bells struck midnight, the two rushed back home. Strangely, Tiny Tim felt like a feather on Bob's shoulders. Close to home, a light snow carpeted the ground. Approaching an icy patch, Bob skidded to give his son a thrill.

"Do it again."

"One more time," laughed Bob. "We shan't be late for our Christmas meal."

Unable to contain his giddiness, Bob skidded several more times on the ice, screaming *wh-e-e-e-e* along with his son.

Giggling with merriment, they arrived home. The smell of the Christmas goose permeated the tiny house. Four children immediately gathered around their father and helped Tiny Tim off his shoulders.

Bob glanced around. "Martha isn't here? I so wanted the family together on this joyous feast to share my news."

When the other children started giggling, Martha popped out from behind the closet door where she was hiding. "Surprise!"

Bob rushed to hug his eldest daughter. "God bless you, Martha." He hugged her again and again, filling his heart with delight. "God bless our family."

Martha hugged her father and the other children joined in with the festival of hugs.

"We have the best family in the whole wide world," beamed Tiny Tim.

"Indeed, we do," said Bob. "And I have the best wife ever."

Emily blushed. "Ye are in a rare mood, Bob Cratchit. But let's sit down before the meal gets cold."

Everyone took their places. Bob's eyes widened as he watched the parade of food being placed on the table—the small baked goose with onion and sage stuffing, mashed potatoes and gravy, and sweet applesauce. That might not have been considered a feast for many, but to the family of eight who rarely left the table with full bellies, the meal represented heavenly abundance.

Before Bob picked up the knife to carve the bird, he asked everyone to hold hands and bow their heads to join in a silent prayer for those in need. After a moment, he joyously proclaimed, "Let's eat!"

Oh, such a clamor of knives and forks as plates were filled and emptied into hungry mouths! Nothing was left of the goose except bones that were picked clean.

Bob patted his tummy. "Though I am stuffed, I have a little room for the Christmas pudding."

That was Emily's cue to bring out the pudding. And what a wonderful pudding it was. Though small as a speckled cannonball, it arrived in a blaze of glory, ignited by brandy with a sprig of Christmas holly stuck on top.

The meal and dessert all done, the dishes were cleared, and coal was placed on the fire. Bob showed Peter how to make his hot punch comprised of water, lemon, a touch of gin, and special spices.

After glasses of punch were served, Bob called to everyone. "Gather round the fireplace. As we roast the chestnuts, I shall tell you a most remarkable story. And every bit is true!"

He held Tiny Tim's withered hand and guided him to a little stool next to him. His wife and other children huddled near the hearth and listened as Bob regaled them with the spellbinding story of Jacob

Marley's visit. The children's mouths opened in astonishment.

He then shared the visitation of Angelica, the tall, vivacious woman with ebony skin, dressed in a flowing red dress decorated with evergreen garlands, exuding the scent of pine. He told them about the scenes he'd visited and the Spirit's message, that he had to learn from the past, then let it go. Only then could he discover his heart's desire.

"I resented my father," he told them. "That kept me a prisoner of the past. I had to forgive him and Uriah Quilp to be free." After pondering that thought a moment, he went on with the story.

He described the bare-footed Noella, the buxom, bawdy Spirit of the Present, exuding the smell of gingerbread. Dressed in a green velvet robe with collar and sleeves trimmed in white fur, her message was clear: Christmas was meant to be celebrated every day. Ignorance and fear stopped people from returning Home to Love. And love was to be shared with everyone.

"Even Scrooge?" asked his eldest son.

"Yes, Peter. Especially Mr. Scrooge," answered his father. "He lives without love so that makes him most in need of it."

Mrs. Cratchit rolled her eyes, not quite accepting that. "He deserves what he dishes out," she added.

"Well, that, my dear Emily, leads me to the Spirit of the Future."

He regaled them about Uriella, the small Asian woman with a purple robe, lavender hair, and a blazing torch that puffed frankincense.

"Her message both excited and frightened me. She told me that my choices affect my future. If my heart's desire is prosperity, and I believe I deserve it, then that is what shall come to us."

He described the stately residence that could be theirs if he truly believed. Mouths dropped lower at that possibility. Everyone *oohed* and *ahhed* about a future that held so much promise.

"I want to play the piano," squealed Belinda, the second eldest daughter.

Bob ruffled her hair. "And so you shall. We shall all hold that desire for you."

Belinda beamed. "I want to play all the Christmas carols."

Her father laughed. "And we shall sing them from the heart!"

"Is the future filled with all good things?" asked Tiny Tim, his face quite solemn. He winced as he moved a leg to get more comfortable.

Bob's heart sank. He did not want to spoil the fun of imagining the stately residence with the lavish furnishings. However, Tiny Tim deserved honesty.

He picked up his son's withered hand. "Tomorrows are made from the choices of today. I may not know what shall come of my choices, but I can choose what to think. What will then come, shall come. Even misfortunes offer opportunities to choose love over fear. As long as we love, we have good fortune."

"What about Tiny Tim's legs?" asked his eldest son.

"That, Master Peter, can be remedied with financial assistance. But we must be vigilant of our thoughts.

That is a small price to pay for the freedom to choose wisely."

"What happens if we forget?" asked Lucy, who was but a year older than Tiny Tim.

Her question cast a pall over the children for they saw their father's face pale.

Wondering whether to talk about Scrooge's death or the cemetery, he chose candor.

"I was shown a horrid future if I did not change my ways. That scene is too horrible to describe." He took a deep breath. "Let me but say that I saw my own and Mr. Scrooge's death."

Emily and her children gasped. "No, that cannot be," cried his wife. She clutched her husband as if he were about to keel over and die.

"Fret not, my dear," he consoled her. "A bleak future appears only when I choose to live in fear. However, I have made a vow to change, for I desire and deserve miracles. Therefore, I shall choose to create a future where love and our family prosper. I shall do my best to make that come true. I promise."

There was a collective sigh of relief from the children terrified at the thought of losing their father.

"There is more to the story," added Bob, wanting to alter the mood.

If the news of the visitations was not shocking enough, Bob mentioned the last encounter with Scrooge. He did not look at his wife when he announced that he was fired. But everyone gasped. Hearing of death was terrifying of itself. Hearing that Bob had lost his job and source of income panicked his wife.

"What shall we do?" cried Emily. "How can we pay our bills?"

Her husband held up his hand. "Do not let fear have its way with us. There is more to the story."

A hush fell over the family.

"Please go on, Father," begged Tiny Tim.

Bob chuckled. "I must confess I worried about our welfare. But my glimpse of the alternative future gave me pause. If Spirits visited me, surely, they would send a sign. And a sign I did receive. When the church bell tolled at ten, I found myself at the home of Mr. Scrooge's nephew. I heard a faint whisper to speak with him, and so I did. I thought I was meant to tell him that Mr. Scrooge needed his assistance since I was no longer in his employ. But my encounter led to an invitation to join his party. There I met some of his wealthy friends, including Albert Bell and Augustus Jingle. They were curious, like Fred, about my departure from Mr. Scrooge."

"The scoundrel," hissed Mrs. Cratchit.

"The story gets better, my dear," soothed her husband. "When they heard I had been fired, they were outraged. Albert Bell cursed Scrooge for not contributing to the Children's Fund and for his greed. He told his friend, Augustus Jingle, that the city needed a firm that would lend money at a just rate. I suggested to them that lending should be fair and reasonable and should help others overcome hardship and prosper. Strangely, both men liked the idea. Mr. Bell consulted with his friend about finding funds to start a lending business. When they asked me if I would manage it, you can imagine my surprise. No sooner had I lost a job when a more lucrative one appeared. I checked around the room to see if Noella was sprinkling her green sparkly stuff but saw no sign of her or the scent of gingerbread. But I daresay, she had a hand in bringing Christmas to me."

"What did you tell them?" asked his awestruck wife.

"Yes, of course." He pulled out coins from his pocket. "They advanced me a small sum to celebrate Christmas."

Emily Cratchit's eyes bulged. She picked the coins out of her husband's hands and inspected them. "They're real!" she exclaimed.

Bob chuckled. "Yes, my dear. A miracle, indeed." He reached over and lifted Tiny Tim's withered hand. "My son, you will get proper treatment."

"Will I be able to walk without braces?"

"I shall hope so," said his father. "And we shall not let fear darken our home." He turned to his oldest son. "And you, Master Peter, shall have a job with the lending business."

Imagining himself a proper man of business, Peter pulled up his collar so high that his ears were not visible.

Bob laughed at the sight of his son wearing his old shirt. "I shall buy you garments that fit properly." He glanced around at the other children whose eyes were wide as saucers. "'Tis time for a toast."

He hoisted a glass of punch. "Merry Christmas. God bless our family!"

Everyone echoed the blessing.

Then Tiny Tim added, "God bless everyone!"

"Indeed!" said Bob. "And that brings us to a special blessing." He raised his glass again. "God bless Mr. Scrooge, the founder of this feast."

"The founder of this feast!" cried Mrs. Cratchit. "The stingy old fool didn't value a good man as ye."

"My dear," said Bob, "remember the Spirits. Each day, we celebrate Christmas. Each day, we spread love and kindness, especially to those in need."

"I'll drink for his health," she said begrudgingly. "But let us give special thanks ye have a new job!"

Everyone clinked their glasses. "Hear, hear."

Bob pointed his glass toward his wife. "To Mother, the loveliest woman in England!"

"Hear, hear," echoed the children.

"Hush," said Emily, blushing beet red.

Bob plucked a sprig of mistletoe from the mantel above the fireplace and held it over his wife. "With you at my side, every day is Christmas." Then he kissed her, causing her face to flush a deeper red.

With so much excitement, the festivities continued for another hour. They shared the jug of punch and roasted chestnuts.

Tiny Tim then led the family in a Christmas song. *"What child is this who lay to rest on Mary's lap is sleeping? Whom angels greet with anthems sweet while shepherds watch are keeping…."*

Because of the excitement, the children did not go to bed until the wee hours. When they finally did, Bob and his wife stayed up and savored another glass of punch. Upon Emily's insistence, he retold the story of the day's events from the very beginning and in greater detail. She marveled at his description of the exact conversation she had had with Belinda in the kitchen earlier that evening. That confirmed to her that Christmas Spirits really had visited.

Both spent long hours talking about the lessons they learned from the past and what they needed to let go so that they could be present to the love around them. Their hearts swelled at the thought of creating a future devoted to spreading glad tidings. They made a vow that should one of them slip into fear, the other would act as a reminder of the presence of love.

When the sun rose, the children woke and found their parents wrapped in each other's arms near the fireplace. The glowing embers kept the room warm.

"It's snowing again," called Tiny Tim, hobbling to the window.

Emily yawned. "I'll put the kettle on the stove for some hot tea."

As the family stirred, the house soon became a hive of activity. Martha, Belinda, and Peter helped in the kitchen. The youngest children—Matthew, Lucy, and Tiny Tim—retrieved the nuts and apples from their stockings, then asked their father to describe the stately residence where they would one day live.

Oh, the fun they had picturing their wildest dreams. However, a sudden rapping on the door broke their reverie.

"Who on earth could that be?" asked Bob.

When he opened the door, a man asked, "Mr. Cratchit?"

"Why, yes."

"Ye have a gift," said the man. He promptly went to the cab and carried in the prize turkey that had been hanging in the poulterer's shop. He handed it to Bob who staggered with the weight of the biggest turkey he had ever seen.

"There must be some mistake," he said.

The man handed Bob a note. "All paid for, sir. Merry Christmas!"

After he left, the children and Emily gathered around Bob, their mouths gaping open. They touched the bird, amazed at the size which was almost as big as Tiny Tim.

"Who sent this?" asked Emily.

Bob shrugged in confusion. Clutching the bird, he gave her the note.

Opening the envelope, Emily read: "To the Cratchit Family. From an old fool who now celebrates this special day. Merry Christmas!"

"It's not signed," she said. "Could it be one of the businessmen from the party?" She showed Bob the note.

He stared at the writing, lost for words.

"What?"

"Though the handwriting is scribbly, I know it to be Mr. Scrooge's."

"Can't be," said his wife.

"Jacob Marley did say he would be visited by Spirits."

"And now this turkey has visited us!" cried Tiny Tim.

As if coming out of a trance, everyone shouted, "Hurrah!"

"Children, all hands to the kitchen," ordered their mother. "We've a feast to prepare."

And a feast the Cratchit family had, one that left every belly fuller than full.

Later that evening, after the dishes were washed, everyone sat around the fire.

Rap. Rap. Rap.

"My goodness," said Emily. "This has been a day of surprises. Who on earth would be coming at this hour?"

When Bob opened the door, he tumbled backward in amazement. Before him stood Ebenezer Scrooge, his arms overflowing with packages.

"Mr. Scrooge! What on earth are you doing here?"

He giggled. "May I come in, Bob? I must relieve my arms of these burdens."

"Why, yes, of course." He raised his eyebrows at his wife who also wondered if Scrooge had been drinking.

Never had he visited their home, but Ebenezer acted as if he had been there before. He placed the packages on the table and gazed at the children's eyes that had grown as large as saucers.

"Ah, such lovely children. Delightful children," he remarked. "And this must be Tiny Tim." He gently ruffled the boy's hair. "Lovely boy. I have something for you and for everyone. The shops were closed, but when I opened my purse, the shopkeepers were all too happy to open their doors."

He laughed heartily as he handed out packages wrapped in brown paper. Each child received a present and looked to the mother for directions. She gave the nod to open them. Each excitedly unwrapped the brown paper. Peter's eyes widened as he found a chess set, and Belinda screamed when she discovered music books. Martha was more constrained but beamed, nonetheless, at the sewing basket filled with needles and threads. Matthew proudly banged on a toy drum, and Lucy cooed over a doll with a frilly pink dress. Tiny Tim waited until his siblings opened their presents before unwrapping his. His eyes widened when he saw the wooden box emblazoned with the word *Thaumatrope*.

"What's a Tomato… rope," he asked, struggling with the word.

Scrooge chuckled and pronounced the word correctly. "A thaumatrope creates an optical illusion. Open the box."

The young boy's hands shook with excitement as he opened the container. Inside, he found twelve cardboard discs with painted pictures. Each disc had strings attached, one to the left side of its picture and another to the right side.

"Go ahead," encouraged Scrooge. "Pick one."

Tiny Tim chose one of the discs. He stared at the picture of a yellow canary on one side, then turned it over to find a picture of an empty birdcage.

"Hold one string with your left fingers and the other string with your right fingers," instructed Scrooge. "Yes. That's it. Now twirl the disc."

With both hands, Tiny Tim began spinning the disc. His eyes widened. "Look! The bird is in the cage!" He gasped, "How did that happen?"

The family *oohed* and *ahhed*.

"That's called an *optical illusion*," Scrooge grinned. "Try another."

This time Tiny Tim chose a disc with a picture of red roses on one side and an empty vase on the other. When he twirled it, he created a vase filled with roses.

That produced more *oohs* and *ahhs* from everyone.

Raising his eyes towards Scrooge, Tiny Tim blinked away tears. "Thank you, Mr. Scrooge." Never before had he, or the other children for that matter, received such special gifts.

Unsure what to make of the generous display, Emily nudged her dumbfounded husband.

"Oh, yes," he said to his children. "What do you say to Mr. Scrooge?"

Almost in unison they yelled, "Thank you, Mr. Scrooge!"

"Remarkable children," giggled Ebenezer. "Delightful children."

"And thank you for the prize turkey," said Bob.

"Oh, yes, Mr. Scrooge," added Emily. "That was very generous of ye. We have plenty of leftovers. Would ye like some?"

"Heavens, no." He patted his stomach. "I'm stuffed from my meal at Fred's house."

"You supped with your nephew?" asked Bob, surprised by the change of events. The day before, he would have nothing to do with a Christmas meal with Fred.

Ebenezer laughed. "I came to my senses, Bob, so to speak." He pointed to a bottle on the table. "I thought you might enjoy some sherry."

Emily protested. "Ye've given more than enough, Mr. Scrooge. We can't take it."

"Nonsense," said the jubilant man. He turned to her husband. "We have much to talk about tomorrow."

"I beg your pardon, sir."

"I'll see you at nine o'clock tomorrow morning."

"Mr. Scrooge, do you not remember? I'm no longer employed."

"Oh, never mind about that. I expect to see you tomorrow."

"I shall come in and complete yesterday's unfinished work. Should only take an hour." He took a deep breath and said, "I'll not be staying after that."

"Let's not talk any further about work on Christmas Day. Tomorrow, we shall have much to talk about. Come in at nine."

He ruffled the hair of each child clutching their gifts. "Remarkable children. Delightful children." He turned to Tiny Tim. "And we shall get you the best medical help."

That comment gave the Cratchits pause. Scrooge was going to help with a cure! The Spirits had, indeed, worked their magic.

"I must be off," he said with a hearty laugh. "I have other errands. More money to give away." He waved his hand to the family. "Merry Christmas!"

The jubilant family echoed the same response. "Merry Christmas, Mr. Scrooge."

The next day, Bob did appear at the lending-house of Scrooge and Marley, albeit eighteen and a half minutes past nine. He found Scrooge sitting behind his desk focused on the papers in front of him.

"Hallo!" growled Scrooge in his accustomed voice. "You were supposed to be here at nine!"

Surprised by the change in tone from the previous day, Bob cautiously approached him. "I was making merry with the bottle of sherry you so generously gave."

"Now, I'll tell you what, my friend," said Scrooge, trying to stifle a giggle. "I am not going to stand this sort of thing any longer. And therefore," he paused then dissolved into laughter. "I am going to raise your salary. Merry Christmas, Bob!" He burst out from behind his desk and gave the man a bear hug.

"Oh, bless you, Ebenezer," rejoiced Bob returning the hug. "I thought you had lost your way again. But now I see that you are right of mind. Merry Christmas!"

"Thank 'ee," he said with a huge smile. "I'll raise your salary and assist your struggling family, and we will discuss your affairs this afternoon, over a bowl of smoking bishop."

Bob placed his hand on Ebenezer's shoulder as if he was an old friend. "I thank you for the offer. I will not say no to mulled wine and friendship, but I must say no to your generous offer of a salary. You see, I shall manage a new business."

Scrooge was taken back by Bob's reply. "You no longer wish to work for me?"

"I am a changed man, like you, Ebenezer. Were you not visited by Jacob Marley and three Spirits?"

Scrooge blinked his eyes, remembering that Bob had foretold him of the visitations on Christmas Eve. "Why, yes."

"I had angelic visitors as well. A new future awaits me and my family. But I shall be honored to create a future with you as my friend."

And lifelong friends they became. From that day forward, people in town wondered about the two miracles that occurred on Christmas. Ebenezer no longer walked the earth a bitter old miser with a closed heart. Instead, he opened his heart and wallet to many. He went on to help Bob establish another lending business. Rather than competing with him, he shared his knowledge so that the community could prosper.

Not only had Scrooge become one of the most generous men in town, but Bob Cratchit moved from poverty to wealth seemingly overnight. He followed his dream of building a business where he and his children worked to create jobs with fair wages so others could break free of poverty. Even sharing his wealth with those in need, he became the most loved soul in town and a stalwart pillar in the community.

Rumor spread that it was Bob who had caused Scrooge's change of heart. Of course, Bob knew otherwise. He and Ebenezer often talked about their encounters with the heavenly apparitions. They kept reminding each other to stay true to their promise to live everyday as Christmas.

As for Tiny Tim, he received the best medical treatment available, compliments of Ebenezer who treated the boy like a nephew. Growing into a healthy young man, Tim would forever sing the praises of his father and his adopted uncle and joyously proclaim, "God bless us, everyone!"

Acknowledgments

Many people have showered me with Christmas presents of support, encouragement, inspiration, and love. It would be impossible to mention them all. However, I send Christmas cheers and thanks to the following people:

My immediate family of my children Melissa and Nate, my sister Rita, my brother Jim, and my deceased sister Marilyn—for all the fond memories of Christmas pasts.

Mary Harris—for her editing and wordsmithing and for keeping me accountable to the book's completion.

Glenda Rynn—for her support, eagle-eyed editing, and wonderful suggestions to uplevel the manuscript.

Ahmed Shaltout—for capturing the essence of the story in the beautiful illustrations.

Tamara Cribley—for designing the polished and professional interior of the book.

Fiona Jayde—for wrapping the book in a delightful cover.

Linda Ulrich-Taylor — for reviewing the manuscript
and offering valuable feedback.

Peter Gray — for being my Aussie friend and
accountability buddy to nudge me over the
finish line.

Pam Sheppard, JJ Flowers, and Jen Myers — for
acting as creative consultants.

My writing critique group of Rick Morgan, Craig
Wells, Dick Hoff, and Mary Keown-Watkins — for
inspiring me to polish, polish, polish.

Larry Porricelli and members of the Southern
California Writers Association — for being part of
my writing community.

Rick Broniec, Steve Pumphrey, Danna Beal, Daniel
Midson-Short, Vladi, Ron Masa, Debbie Hart, Gail
Mor, Paul McBryde, Mari Frank, Jim Lee, Ginger
Szymczak, Brandon Hall, Arthur Tassinello, Kevin
O'Connor, and Catherine Clinch — for their encour-
agement and support.

Finally, to my family, friends, and fellow writers —
for continually encouraging me to stay present
with the spirit of Christmas. I thank you all!

Merry Christmas!

The Miracles of Christmas
Continue in

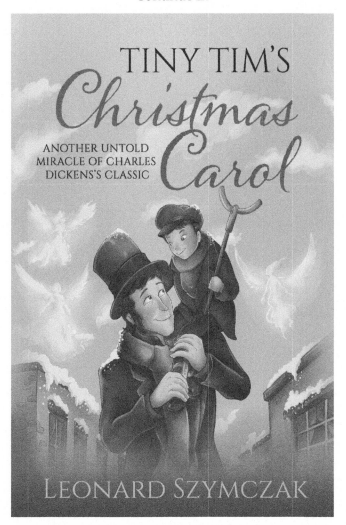

TINY TIM'S
Christmas

ANOTHER UNTOLD
MIRACLE OF CHARLES
DICKENS'S CLASSIC *Carol*

LEONARD SZYMCZAK

Chapter One

Tiny Tim

In a rundown part of London in 1843, Tiny Tim, as his parents referred to him, woke up before everyone else on Christmas Eve. The six-year-old boy felt cramped in the bed that he shared with his two brothers — Matthew, older by a year, and Peter who at eleven was the eldest boy in the family. Wincing with pain, Tim slowly wriggled his way to the edge of the bed, not an easy task. Having been born with a medical condition that made his bones soft and weak, his body ached with every movement.

"Go back to sleep," whispered Peter. "It's still dark."

Despite the pain, Tim gushed, "It's Christmas Eve!"

"Barely," said Peter.

"Grrr." Matthew elbowed Tim in his ribs. "Quit talkin'."

"Ouch," cried Tim, an undersized boy, pale and bony. When Matthew, sandwiched between his brothers, elbowed him again, this time more fiercely, Tim yelped.

"Cut it out," hissed Peter.

While Tim avoided conflict, the hot-tempered seven-year-old Matthew did not. He resented the attention that Tim received because of his malady. As the fifth of six children, Matthew grumbled about being overlooked and took it out on his brother. That only made others feel sorrier for Tim, who rarely complained. This infuriated Matthew. A stronger and healthier boy, he mercilessly picked on his brother when his parents weren't around.

Elbowing Tim in the ribs again, Matthew growled. "Grrr. You're wakin' me."

"Stop it!" hissed Peter.

Tim slid off the crowded bed and quickly relieved himself in the chamber pot. He then started the arduous task of dressing himself in his worn and patched black trousers and oversize grey shirt. Wincing in pain, he put on the threadbare hand-me-downs from Matthew who had received them from Peter. The oversized clothes made him look even tinier.

He grimaced when he fastened the iron leg braces to his pant legs that were reinforced with heavy patches to prevent the metal from wearing through the fabric. While the braces enabled him to walk, he still needed a scruffy wooden crutch for added support. Any tumble took a savage toll on his frail bones and caused excruciating pain, so he took extra care whenever he moved.

Though his body throbbed most of the time, he rarely complained aloud. Sympathy was the last thing that Tiny Tim sought. He didn't want anyone to worry, especially his father who carried the weight of responsibility as the provider of the large family. Yet, even with that burden, Bob Cratchit treated his son with loving kindness, carrying him on his shoulders whenever they left the house.

Hobbling toward the stone-cold fireplace, Tim glanced at the window not yet illuminated by the rising sun. He shivered as he waited for his father to wake up and start a fire.

The tiny four-room house was the only home Tim had ever known. With one small room as the kitchen, another served as the hub of the house with the fireplace and dining table. Two other rooms were converted into bedrooms, one for Tim and his two brothers and the other for his three sisters and his parents, though his mother had strung a curtain to separate the girls from their parents' bed.

"Up so early," whispered his father.

Tim's eyes widened. "'Tis Christmas Eve!"

Bob Cratchit ruffled his son's unruly mop of brown hair. "Indeed! And a very fine Christmas we shall have!"

The sight of Tiny Tim waiting for him by the fireplace warmed Bob's heart. He felt a close bond with his son as a kindred spirit, for both put on a brave face when confronted with hardship.

A short man with unkempt black hair and muttonchop sideburns, Bob kissed the top of Tim's head. "Let's get some coals burning, shall we?"

His son's tiny hand reached down and grasped a lump of coal from the bin.

Bob remarked, "You've chosen a fine piece of coal, indeed."

Even though all the lumps looked the same, his father's typical comment brought a smile to Tim's face.

Completing their early morning ritual, Bob cleared the debris from last night's fire. He then placed Tim's lump of coal at the center of the fireplace and surrounded it with chunks of coal. Then he repeated the same prayer along with his son that they uttered every morning.

"May the light of God be with us today," they said in unison.

With the lighting of the fire complete, Tim asked, "Father, can you come home early today? 'Tis Christmas Eve!"

Bob thought of his employer and cringed. Ebenezer Scrooge reviled Christmas, so much so that the miser piled on extra work to make up for Bob's absence on the holiday.

"I'm afraid I'll have to work late, son."

"Maybe Mr. Scrooge will let you leave early."

Bob sighed. "I'm afraid not." Having worked for Scrooge for twenty long years for scant compensation, Bob knew him as a coldhearted man who greedily managed his wealth and possessions even down to the bucket of coal. He was lucky to burn one lump at a time as Scrooge never indulged in excess. preferring a frosty office.

"I must get ready," said Bob, his shoulders slouching. "It will be a very long day, indeed."

Tim placed a withered hand on his father's arm. "I pray for a miracle, Father, that Mr. Scrooge treats you kindly."

Bob patted his son's head. "'Tis Christmas. Never you worry."

But Tim did worry. About the pain that was getting worse and about getting bullied by his brother and the others in the neighborhood. But he mostly worried about his father who, like Tim, rarely complained. Even though his father maintained a brave front for a life of servitude and misery at work, Tim, the ever-sensitive soul, did not miss the slouched shoulders, furrowed brow, and exhausted look when his father returned home from work.

Following his father's example, Tim did not complain. Walking a few steps often brought intense agony, even with the support of braces and a crutch. He kept his pain to himself and portrayed a demeanor of optimism, not daring to tell anyone about the thoughts of death plaguing him daily and sometimes into the night when monsters appeared in his dreams.

To read more, visit leonardsz.com.

ABOUT THE AUTHOR

 Leonard Szymczak is an award-winning author, TEDx speaker, psychotherapist, and life coach. His books include *The Roadmap Home: Your GPS to Inner Peace*, an Amazon bestseller, and the lighthearted satires on psychotherapy *Cuckoo Forevermore* and the award-winning *Kookaburra's Last Laugh*, lighthearted satires on psychotherapy. He is the co-author, along with Mari Frank, of *Fighting for Love: Turn Conflict into Intimacy*.

In September 2019 Leonard delivered a TEDx talk viewed by 100K, "In the Age of Superheroes, Where Are the Fathers?" He lives in Southern California where he writes, coaches clients, and conducts seminars. He is the proud father of two adult children and three grandchildren.

For more information about Leonard's books, seminars, speaking engagements, coaching, or free downloads, you can contact him or visit his websites at:

leonardsz.com
leonard@leonardsz.com
twitter.com/lszymczak
fb.com/leonardszymczakauthor

NOTE FROM THE AUTHOR

Thanks for reading *Bob Cratchit's Christmas Carol*.
If you enjoyed this book, please consider leaving a
review online at your favorite store's website.
May the Christmas Spirit always be with you.

Leonard Szymczak

Made in the USA
Las Vegas, NV
17 December 2022

63074837R00069